ESCAPE KIT

ESCAPE KIT

WILLIAM THIRSK-GASKILL

Grist Books 2014

Editor Michael Stewart

Editorial Team Jai Edge, Sarah Milne, Kate Pearson, James Whitely

Cover Design Kagayaku Ink

Inner Page Design Carnegie Book Production

Escape Kit is published by Grist Books.

Please note that all work published here is previously unpublished.

www.hud.ac.uk/grist

Copyright © William Thirsk-Gaskill 2014

All rights reserved

Grist Books is supported entirely by The University of Huddersfield and would not exist without this support. We would like to take the opportunity to express our gratitude for this continuing support.

ISBN: 978-0-9563099-4-5

Dedicated to Flight Lieutenant Philip Ainsworth Gaskill, and Lance Corporal William John Christie Anderson, in recognition of military service and many other things.

Contents

1. Escape Kit   1
2. Extra German   7
3. Keep Calm   13
4. Return from Heidelberg   23
5. Suspect Device   31

1. Escape Kit

I'VE GOT A parcel from the Red Cross. I've been expecting it for ages. You'll never guess what it is, so I'll tell you. It's a Monopoly set. Have a look at it if you like. Seems perfectly ordinary, doesn't it? Examine it, especially the board. You know the thing that kids always say when they play Monopoly. 'Wouldn't it be amazing if all this money was real?' They always say that, don't they? Well, where this particular Monopoly set is concerned, there would be a kind of irony if you said that. No, no, the money is as fake as with any other. You can tell that just by looking at it. The notes are too small to be real money, for a start. They've only got printing on one side, no thread – completely childish. It is the board you should be looking at. It's full of banknotes. Real banknotes. Reichsmarks, French francs, Swiss francs. All real. And the square-heads have no idea. You have to cut the board open to find them. I bet every Monopoly set sent to British prisoners of war has been used to smuggle currency. Ha ha. When we get one over on them like that, it does you good, you know. Helps you to keep going.

This place could be a lot worse, I suppose, but being cooped up by a lot of square-heads does get you down, sometimes, especially now, when it's winter. It isn't just the cold, though I don't think I really knew what cold was until I was brought here. It's Christmas at home that I miss. Christmas with Mildred – that's my Mrs – and the kids, Timothy and Mary. Timothy will be nine, now, and Mary's six.

At least we are reasonably well-off for food. We get that from the Red Cross as well. We are very careful with it and we have managed to save enough up for a little celebration. Tea, coffee, chocolate, condensed milk – the lot. Tommy Freeborn – I always think that name is particularly inappropriate for a Prisoner of War – old Tommy Freeborn says he has saved up enough dried fruit and enough sugar to make us a cake. He is short of flour, but he says that will be all right, because he can use breadcrumbs, bound together with powdered egg. That might sound a bit unappetising, but I tell you, Tommy is a good cook. If he says it will taste like Christmas cake, then you can be sure it will. He's wondering if the next parcel will contain any marzipan. Hope springs eternal, I suppose.

I sincerely hope that I won't be needing the French francs. I've got my route worked out already. I bet you're wondering how I did that. I am not a whizz at geography – I always hated it in school, almost as much as Latin – no, I've got a map. It came in the last Red Cross parcel, hidden inside a set of gramophone records. Beethoven's Symphony Number 3, 'The Eroica'. The camp Kommandant noticed the box, and asked what it was. When we told him, he said he was delighted that we were willing to be enlightened by German culture. Ha! Little does he suspect that the first thing we did with them once we got the chance was to smash them all, to get the pieces of the map out. I've gummed them all together, and I've got the whole route planned, from where we are now, that's here, in eastern Germany, to here, which is Basel, near the German-Swiss border. Once I get out of the camp – that's the easy bit – I'll have to get to the nearest large town, or at least the nearest railway station. I'm hoping that if I can get to Berlin, or Magdeburg, or Dresden, I should be able to get a train all the way to Basel. The square-heads will stop the train, of course, before it crosses the border into Switzerland but, once I'm inside a neutral country, I'm safe. No, if I end up having to spend any French francs, it will probably mean that something has gone horribly wrong.

The way I'm going to get out is by climbing down a rope. There's a window in a room upstairs which is used as a chapel, and the square-heads have not bothered to put bars over it because there is such a large drop underneath. I've measured it by dangling a piece of cotton with a plumb-bob on the end out of the window. I had to wind the cotton back up and give it back to the Quartermaster when I had finished – it is 'waste not, want not' in here – but I measured the cotton, and I can tell you that the distance from the windowsill to the ground is fifty-eight feet, six-and-a-half inches. I've got a hundred and twenty feet of rope, which I made by plaiting together four washing-lines and some cord made of strips cut off the edges of bed-sheets. I stitched these together first, to make them stronger. I've tested it, and it seems to have enough breaking-strain. Well, it had better do. The problem I am working on now is how to get down the rope. One of the chaps who is a Commando says he can teach me how to abseil. That's why I need a hundred and twenty feet of rope to get down a sixty-foot drop: you need a double strand of rope if you are going to abseil.

Once I reach the ground, assuming I am still in one piece, I have to get through the wire. Wire-cutters are like gold dust because, unlike the rope, they are very tricky for the chaps you leave behind to retrieve after you have used them. There is supposed to be a gentleman's agreement that you lob them as hard as you can back into the camp, once you are through, but I would not blame a chap for not doing that. If they landed anywhere near one of the goons, you would be giving away the fact that you were escaping. Besides, it would be odds-on that a goon would find them before one of us did, and so what would be the good of that? I keep telling people that running out of wire-cutters is a nice problem to have, because it means that they have all been put to good use.

No, getting down the wall and through the wire are not the parts that concern me, because they are just me against something physical. That is the kind of challenge I was trained for. The thing I have to worry about is anything that involves dealing with the enemy, especially speaking to them in German. I have spent hours and hours mugging up on German, but it has been a bit of a struggle. I didn't do it at my school. I wish I had done German instead of Latin. Even if you manage to keep your accent right, and use the right phrases to ask for your train ticket, or whatever it is you are doing, there is always the chance that someone will ask you a question. 'Wasn't it terrible when the opera house was hit in the air-raid last week?' and of course you agree, but it turns out to have been a trick question: there was no air-raid last week, or the town doesn't have an opera house. I've decided that the only thing to do is to say as few words as possible. I would much rather people took me for someone who is surly, or a bit touched in the head, than for a PoW trying to escape. If somebody tries to make small-talk with me, I am just going to think about a brick wall.

It is an idea I got from a film I saw once. Can't remember what it was called. Something about The Damned. There was this chap who was in a room with some ghastly-looking children who could read his mind. To save the village, and the world, he had to blow them up, with a time-bomb he had in his briefcase. But he couldn't allow himself to think about the time-bomb, not even for a second, and so he trained himself to think about a brick wall. I think that is quite clever, because it is so much easier than thinking about nothing.

I hope I don't end up having to do away with myself. I do have an I-capsule. That is a little thing containing a concentrated solution of potassium cyanide, in case you didn't know. Not that there is anything I could tell Jerry that he doesn't already know, having been cooped in here for such a long time. I also have another form of insurance policy that I'd rather not explain, not even to you.

I think my escape kit is pretty well complete, now my Monopoly set has arrived. Rope, wire-cutters, currency, civilian disguise, false Reich passport in the name of Karl-Heinz Weber, rations, compass, map, and that other little thing I perhaps should not have mentioned. Yes, I think I am just about ready to go. I'm going to climb out of the chapel window at 0600, just as they are changing the guard. It'll still be dark, then.

I've made it down the wall with no bones broken, and I'm through the wire. No hitch at all. Now to get to the railway station. It's about four miles, but I think I'll walk it. That'll be safer.

Made it. Here I am at the station. I'm checking the departure timetable. Ah. There aren't any trains to Basel from here. The nearest to Basel I can get from this station seems to be London Kings Cross. I'll have to get to Switzerland via King's Cross. Good job I have still got some sterling with me.

2. Extra German

My name is Bradley Crichton. I'm fourteen years old. This is the first time I have been on a train on my own. I am going to visit my grandparents in Stevenage. I'm getting on at York. I have a seat reserved in coach F, seat 23A. The train stops at Doncaster, Retford, Newark Northgate, Grantham, Peterborough, and then Stevenage. Six stops. And then it goes on to London Kings Cross, and so I have to make sure I get off at Stevenage. My grandpa is supposed to be picking me up at the station. I am going to see my grandparents while my dad is attending a modern language conference at Heidelberg University. That's in Germany. My mum will still be at home, but she says she's busy with some work, and wants peace and quiet. My sister doesn't live at home any more. She and my dad had a big row just before she went to university. She doesn't even come home during the holidays, and I miss her, even though we used to argue all the time when she lived with us. I told my mum I would be very quiet if she just let me stay at home, but she kept telling me I would enjoy being with grandma and grandpa once I got there. I hope she's right. I think she just wanted to get me out of the house. In some ways, I'll be glad to go for a while, even though there is nothing to do at grandma's house other than eat or watch television. My mother's been really strange, recently, and my dad's been away for ages. He told me he was going to a conference, but it seems to be lasting for weeks.

I have found my seat. I am sure this is the right seat. This is definitely coach F. The seat is in a group of four with a table in the middle. I am next to the window. I put my suitcase on the luggage rack. It isn't too heavy. I'm only going for three days. There is a man sitting in the seat opposite mine. The other two seats are empty.

The man is quite old. I think he must be about seventy. Or maybe sixty. It is difficult to tell. Maybe late forties. He has little, watery eyes, and he keeps glancing in different directions. He looks at me for a second, after I have sat down, and I look at him and smile, but he looks away again straight away. He doesn't smile. He looks nervous. Perhaps he is worried that he has got on the wrong train, or hasn't got the right sort of ticket. His clothes look funny. They look like he made them himself. They look like bits of old clothes that have been cut up and sewn together again, all mixed-up. His coat seems too big for him. He's wearing a funny kind of hat with a peak. It looks a bit like that Greek fisherman's cap that my older sister used to wear, but not as trendy. He's got a duffle-bag with him. I don't know what he's got in it.

I am just about to ask him if he needs any information about the train, when I hear the doors closing. I look at my watch and see that it is setting off exactly on time. There is no point in asking him if he is sure he is on the right train now, because it's too late. I suppose he will find out when the ticket inspector comes round.

I read my book for a while. It is 'King Solomon's Mines' by H. Rider Haggard. It is a very exciting story, but

I can't get into it properly, because I am worried about the man. I think I need to say something to him. I don't usually say things to people I don't know.

'Are you going all the way to London Kings Cross?' I ask him. He looks at me as if I have just said something really horrible. He keeps opening his mouth, as if he is about to say something, but no words come out. And then he says, 'Ich reise nach Basel.' The words he speaks mean, 'I travel towards Basel', but he says it in German. He doesn't look German, but perhaps he is. Maybe that is why he is nervous. Maybe he is German, and can't understand much English. He must be able to understand some English, because he answered my question. If he is going to Basel, perhaps he's Swiss. One of the people my mum works with is Swiss, and she comes from near Basel. But she speaks fluent English, even really bad swear-words.

'My name is Bradley Crichton. I live in Pocklington. I also go to school in Pocklington. I learn German at school, and also with my tutor. My father is a translator,' I say, all in German. He looks at me. He still doesn't look happy. 'I have a sister. She is called Katrina. She is nineteen years old. I am fourteen years old.' I start with this sort of stuff because it is easy to say and I know it all off by heart. I am beginning to think that those extra German lessons my mum makes me have are finally coming in useful. But something else strikes me as weird, which is that if this guy is German or Swiss, it is unusual that he feels so unsure about speaking English. Maybe he didn't have a very good education.

'Lassen Sie mich allein, bitte,' he says. 'Leave me alone, please,' but with an English accent. The word for 'you' he pronounces as 'see', instead of 'zee'. The word for 'me' he says like 'Mick', instead of making the 'ch' sound in his throat, like Scottish people do. I don't get this at all, even though he pronounces 'please' as 'bitter' rather than 'bit'. He understands what I say to him in English, but he only replies in German, and he speaks with a noticeably English accent. I'd get marked down if I pronounced German words the way he does. German pronunciation is pretty easy, once you have got the hang of it. There are loads of things, like the stuff my dad translates, that I can read aloud in German so that it sounds correct, but don't know the meaning of all of it.

'Entschuldigung. Ich halte jezt ruhig,' I say, which means 'Sorry. I keep quiet now'. For a moment, he breathes out, and stops fidgeting, and then he puffs his chest out a bit, and leans towards me, with his elbows on the table.

I can't believe what he just said. This guy must be mad. He just asked me, 'Sie sind Hitler-Jugend?' That means, 'Are you Hitler Youth?' I am so shocked, that all I can think of to say is, 'Nein, überhaupt nicht,' which means, 'No, definitely not.' He shakes his head, and accuses me of lying. He asks me if I am going to talk to the police about him. He doesn't say, 'Polizei', which is the word I would use for 'police'. He says 'Gestapo', like the Nazis had during the Second World War. I happen to know that it stands for Geheime Staatspolizei and it means 'Secret State Police'. We did it in history last term, but my dad says it as well. If he finds me doing something that we both know will make my mum do her nut, he says he is going to report me to the Geheime Staatspolizei.

'Es gibt kein Gestapo hier,' I say. My throat is drying up. As I say it, I think he might not hear me. Then I think that I shouldn't try to contradict him.

'Ha!' he replies. 'Ich glaube nein. Achtung!' 'I don't think so. Look out!' And then he fumbles in his inside pocket, and he pulls out a Luger pistol, and points it at me. I know it is a Luger, because I used to have one for my Action Man storm-trooper. It is very easy to recognise. The barrel of the pistol is black and shiny. It looks as if it is covered in oil. He holds it with both hands. I can see that his hands are shaking. I can't decide if I want someone to pass by and see him, or not. I want someone to come and help, but I don't want him to panic. Even though he is shaking, he can't miss at this range. He is aiming right for my heart. I start to shake as well. My teeth start to chatter.

'Bitte nicht scheissen. Bitte nicht scheissen,' I say, over and over again. It is an easy enough phrase to know how to say. I have heard phrases like it in films, but I never thought I would have to say it for real.

'Ruhe! Spracht nicht kein Erlaubnis,' he says, which kind of means 'Be quiet. Don't talk without permission.' I nod about ten times.

'Kann ich schlafen gehen, jetzt, bitte?' 'Can I go to sleep now, please?' I ask him, and put my hands together by the side of my head to make sure he understands.

'Gut. Ja,' is all he says, and he puts the Luger back in his inside pocket.

I take my coat off the seat beside me, and put it over my head, like a blanket. I can feel my own warm breath in the dark space under the coat, but I still feel cold all over. I try to tell myself that I am not having a gun pointed at me any more. But I can't stop thinking about the Luger. I wonder how many bullets he has in the magazine. I can't remember how many bullets a Luger takes. It's probably seven. Or maybe nine. Or eight.

Moving my hands as slowly and as gently as possible, I unzip the inside pocket of my coat. I move the zip one tooth at a time, so it doesn't make any sound. It takes me about two minutes to open the pocket, but it seems like two hours. I get out my mobile phone. The moment I take it out of the pocket, the screen starts to glow. My friend, Jake, is ringing me. I set the phone to silent, just in time to mute the call. I decline the call. I text my mum.

> 6 Dec 2012 10:06
> Hi mum. I am on the train to grandma's. There is a madman sitting opposite me with a Luger pistol. He thinks I am a member of the Hitler Youth. He thinks I am going to sleep under my coat now. He is going to Kings Cross. I am worried that he won't let me off the train at Stevenage. And I'm a bit worried that he might shoot me. Help. Love, Bradley. P.S. I am not kidding. P.P.S. He only speaks German. I'm sorry I complained when you made me do extra German lessons.

3. Keep Calm

I HAVE JUST nearly crashed my car after glancing at a text message from my son. Celia Jane Crichton, that will teach you not to faff about with your phone while you are driving. Or perhaps it won't, because I'm glad that I saw the message as soon as Bradley had sent it. I've pulled into a side-street and I'm re-reading the message. I don't know this area. I've never been here before. It's always that, whenever you're in a place you don't know, and you need to turn the car round or pull over, it takes you ages to find somewhere. All you ever get is a straight road, and somebody right behind you driving right up your arse. Anyway, I am on a street called Palmerston Crescent. The sat nav keeps telling me to turn round at the first opportunity.

What on earth should I make of Bradley's text? If it's a joke, then it's much more elaborate than I would have thought Bradley capable of. Bradley tends to live in the world of the literal and the here-and-now. Dreaming up an imaginary madman with a gun is not his style, though it's definitely like Bradley to mention that it's a Luger and not any other kind of gun. The thing that clinches it is the bit about being glad that I made him do extra German. He seethed with resentment when I told him about that, and came up with every method he could think of to try to make me feel bad about it. This message doesn't look like a joke. Oh, dear. I think I may be starting to have a panic attack.

> 6 Dec 2012 10:14
> Hi Brad. Keep calm and don't do anything sudden. Don't worry about staying on train past Stevenage. Just try to keep calm and keep safe. I'll call police, grandpa, and your dad. Be brave but be calm and sensible. I love you.
> XXXX Mum.

The next thing I do is to call Davina. I call her mobile, but it goes straight through to voicemail. I thought I had the number of the hotel in my phone, but I can't find it. I look up the number on the internet, ring the reception desk, and ask to be put through to Davina Dawson. It takes her ages to answer. When someone picks up, it is the receptionist again. I ask her to check that Ms Dawson has checked in, which she has, and ask to be put through again. This time, Davina answers.

'Hello?'

'Hello, Davina? It's me, Celia.'

'Are you on your way? Where are you?'

'Yes, I'm on my way. I set off about twenty minutes ago. I can't talk for more than a minute. I've had a text from Bradley. He's in trouble. I've got to make some calls.'

'Calls to who? What sort of trouble?'

'Well, to the police for a start, and then to my father – and to Edmund, I suppose.'

'I thought we had agreed that you weren't going to have any further communication with Edmund, other than through a recognised intermediary.'

'Well, yes, we did.'

'And?'

'This won't be "communication" in the two-way sense. I just need to let him know something's happened to Bradley. I'll be there as quick as I can, but I can't talk now. I have to make some important calls. I'll be there as quick as I can. Bye.'

'What has happened to Bradley?'

'I'll call you back as soon as I've dealt with the situation. Bye.'

I knew something like this would happen. I knew something unexpected would blow up and threaten to wreck my plans. Anyway, I can't think about that now. I need to call the police. How do you get the police on a mobile? Is it 999, or 112? Well, at least it seems to be ringing.

I can't remember much about what I said to the emergency services switchboard operator, certainly not beyond, 'Which service do you require?' I went blank for a moment after I had said the word 'police', because I started thinking about ambulances, and paramedics, and gunshot wounds and arterial bleeding. They asked me which train he was on, and I could remember that it was going to Kings Cross and stopping at Stevenage, of course, but I couldn't remember what time it had left York. All I could remember was what time I had dropped Bradley off, which was about a quarter to ten.

Oh, god, my phone is getting low on charge. My car-charger broke three weeks ago, and I havn't got round to buying another one yet.

> 8 December 2012 10:21
> Brad, I've called the police. They will
> deal with it. Try not to worry. My phone
> is dying and I won't be able to charge it
> for a while. I'll ring from a landline to
> make sure you are all right. Love, Mum.
> X

The one thing I remember to do before the phone battery gets any lower is to bring up Bradley's mobile number and write it down. I am just starting to feel guilty about not knowing it from memory but then I think nobody has memorised numbers since mobiles were invented. I stop feeling guilty about Bradley's phone number, and then I realise that the scrap of paper I have written it down on is the receipt for the two bottles of sparkling wine I bought out of this month's housekeeping money to share with Davina.

> 8 December 2012 10:32
> Davina, my phone is dying. I'll be there
> as quick as I can. Love, C. xXXXx

I decide to risk the last bit of charge on calling Edmund. I don't owe him anything, but it seems the right thing to do and it might make me feel better, depending on what condition he is in.

He picks up immediately. I don't even hear the ringtone. That is probably a good sign.

'Hello?' says Edmund, before I have even had a chance to say anything. 'Celia, are you there? I've had a ghastly text from Bradley. He's on a train, and there's some madman threatening him with a gun. I've called the police.'

'Yes, so have I.'

'Well thank god for that. Maybe if they match the two calls, they'll take it seriously. How are you feeling? I don't know what to do. I feel so helpless. How long do you think it'll be before the police decide to do anything?'

'I don't know, Edmund. I expect it will seem to take a lot longer than it actually does. I'm just glad that you know what the situation is.'

'Yes. Terrible.'

'Edmund?'

'What?'

'Why are you sober?'

'I've been sober for fifteen days. I've started going to meetings. It seems to be working.'

'Oh, good.'

'I've landed a big chunk of work to do as well, which helps enormously.'

'Oh, well done. Who is it for? What sort of thing is it?'

I don't know what Edmund said in response, because the phone gave out at that point. I realise that I have not yet rung my father. I'm not going to worry about that. I can ring him from the hotel, and there isn't a damned thing he can do to help, at least until we've heard from the police. He does tend to worry, and my mother's even worse.

I can't remember the last time Edmund was sober. It must have been over a year ago. Davina told me only to communicate with him through a go-between, such as my solicitor or 'a trained professional'. That is her code for 'therapist', which means her. It used to mean her. That is how we met. There was a rapport between us from the very first session. Davina was living with a partner at that time. She did not say much about her home life at first. When she did, I gathered that she had problems of her own. She kept telling me to 'be honest'. She really meant honest about my relationship with Edmund. I suppose she was trying to get me to admit that he is an alcoholic. It took me a very long time, but eventually I summoned up the courage to ask her why I had to carry on paying her sixty pounds per fifty-minute session to listen to her talking about her own problems. She said, 'You don't. We could go to a pub and you could listen to them for free.' I thought she was having a go at me, but in fact she was asking me out.

We've been on three dates now, including once to the pictures and once to see a play. She isn't my therapist anymore, of course, because of professional ethics. We do seem good together, and we've had a lot of fun, but we haven't slept together yet. I wanted everything to be stable and sorted. I didn't want to have to worry about some bizarre crisis with Bradley, or whether I'm a bad mother for letting him take the train on his own, or being late to meet Davina, or why Edmund is sober for the first time in ages, or what his being sober might mean. Well, there is nothing to do other than keep going. At least I know I am not going to run out of petrol.

I don't believe it. There is a phone box and a lay-by. I'm pulling over.

The phone box is actually working, and I've got bags of change. There is no phone book, like there would have been in the old days. Can I remember the number of the hotel? Don't think, just punch the number in. Somebody answers. Yes. They are putting me through to Davina's room again.

'Hello?'

'Davina, it's Celia again. My mobile has died but I'm calling you from a phone box. I'm on my way but I just wanted to let you know straight away what the situation is. It's Bradley.'

'Yes, you said. What about Bradley?'

'He's on the train to his grandparents' house. He sent me a text to say that there is a nutter sitting opposite, who is pointing a gun at him.'

'A gun.'

'Yes. He said it was a Luger.'

'A Luger.'

'Yes.'

'A real gun?'

'Well, he didn't say, but then I wouldn't expect him to know that. Is that important? Wouldn't you be scared at fourteen even if somebody was pointing what turned out to be a toy gun at you, if it looked real?'

'What sort of person is this nutter? Did Bradley give any details about him?'

'Well the message was understandably brief but he said he thought he was a member of the Hitler Youth.'

'Bradley thinks this nutter is a member of the Hitler Youth. So he's a young nutter, then? In a brown shirt and lederhosen, with a swastika armband?'

'No. Bradley said that the nutter said that he – Bradley – was a member of the Hitler Youth.'

'And is Bradley now, or has Bradley ever been, a member of the Hitler Youth?'

'Davina, you are not making this situation any easier. This is serious. I am desperately worried. I've called the police. So has Edmund.'

'You've been speaking to Edmund?'

'Edmund is the boy's father. He was sober, as a matter of fact. He was quite sensitive about it. He's as cut-up as I am.'

'I see. Edmund is being sober and sensitive. That seems like remarkably good timing.'

'I just wanted to let you know what's happening.' Davina doesn't say anything. There is a long pause. 'I've brought some wine, and some of the things you asked me to bring. Not all of them. But some.' Another pause. 'I'll be there as quick as I can.' I put some more money into the coin-slot. That seems a silly thing to do, since I just want to put the phone down and get back on the road. 'I'll have to ring the police again when I get there and leave them the Deer Park hotel's number.' There is another slight pause, but then Davina does speak again.

'Celia, why are you saying all that when it is blatantly obvious that you aren't coming?'

'What?'

'Any fool can see that you aren't coming. You are just playing for time.'

'I'm on my way.'

'Don't lie to me. And for goodness' sake, don't try to insult my intelligence with some pathetic, childish story about a gunman on a train. We are both grown-ups, and we both know that there is no gunman, there is no Luger, and there is no train.'

'There is a train. I dropped him off at the station myself this morning.'

'Give me a break. What I'm saying is that the substance of the story is rubbish, and half-arsed rubbish at that. I think we will have to file this one under "Could Do Better". If you weren't ready for a physical relationship, why could you not simply have done the honest thing and said so, instead of coming out with all this? And by the way, I will be expecting you to pay the hotel bill, since it is you who has ruined the weekend. I think that's only fair. It cost extra for the early check-in.'

'Davina, I don't know what to say, other than, "I'm on my way".'

'Well, when you get here, the room will be empty. I hope you enjoy your stay.'

'What?'

'I'm leaving. I've had enough of this. You can do the checking out. I thought I had really succeeded with you. I thought I had managed to turn a self-deluding jelly into a thinking, seeing, listening, independent, honest human being. I see now that I failed. Goodbye, Celia.'

She puts the phone down. I feel hollow and half-asleep. I'm not sure I can drive in this state. I leave unspent coins in the slot. I leave the receiver dangling by the metal-coated wire. I get back in the car and just sit. I don't know what to do. If it weren't for the danger that Bradley is in, I don't think I would be able to feel anything. I have no idea how much the hotel bill is going to be, or much idea how I am going to pay it.

I wish Ed was here.

4. Return from Heidelberg

I RING MY estranged wife back as soon as we get cut off, just in case it's a blip in the signal. It goes through to voicemail.

'Celia, it's Edmund. Ring me back straight away, please.' I wait a couple of minutes for her to plug the phone-charger in, and call again. Still voicemail. I can't understand it. Maybe she's talking to the police.

> 8 December 2012 10:41
> Brad, this is Dad. Are you still OK?

>> 8 December 2012 10:43
>> I'm fine. I'm still pretending to be asleep. The man doesn't know I'm texting. Are you still in Heidelberg?

> 8 December 2012 10:47
> No, son. I'm in Pocklington. I have not been in Heidelberg recently. That is something me and your mother made up. I'm really sorry.

8 December 2012 10:51
Why?

8 December 2012 10:56
I needed some time alone so that I could stop drinking. Then it'll be up to your mother to decide if I can move back home. I'll always be your dad, of course.

8 December 2012 11:01
Have you stopped drinking?

8 December 2012 11:03
All I can say is that I have not had any alcohol for 15 days. I have started going to meetings, which help me to want to stay off drink, and I've got a big piece of work in. I have to stay sober to get the work done. Lack of work was one reason I started drinking heavily.

8 December 2012 11:07
What was another reason?

8 December 2012 11:09
I thought your mother didn't love me.

8 December 2012 11:11
I am sure she does love you dad but I also think she might be seeing someone else.

8 December 2012 11:14
I was afraid she might be. I don't blame

her. That's something me and your
mum will have to sort out.

> 8 December 2012 11:18
> I think I know who it is.

8 December 2012 11:19
Who?

8 December 2012 11:20
Son? Are you there?

8 December 2012 11:23
Brad, are you all right?

8 December 2012 11:26
What's happening, son?

I call Celia. I can't think of anything else to do. She answers this time.

'Hello.'

'Celia, what's the matter? You sound as if you've been crying. Have the police called? Is there any news?'

'No, the police haven't called. It's not Bradley. I'm upset about something else. I know it isn't important compared to Bradley, but it's caught me off-guard.'

'What is it?'

'I can't talk about it at the moment.'

'Okay.'

'Since you ask, I've been dumped.'

'Dumped?'

'By a woman. In a particularly vindictive and humiliating way. And I may get a bill for a hotel room that no-one is staying in for one hundred and sixty-nine pounds and ninety-nine pence that I haven't got the money to pay. And I'm alone in an empty house. And my son is being held at gunpoint on a train, and I'm not there to protect him.'

'Celia, have you been drinking?'

'Yes. Lukewarm Rosado Cava out of the bottle. Why? Don't you approve?'

'I was just asking. And I know what a bad idea it is to drink when you're depressed.' Celia doesn't speak. I can hear her swigging the fizzy wine out of the bottle. I can imagine exactly what it would feel and taste like, and it makes me feel sick. 'Celia, I've told Bradley about Heidelberg.'

'I know that. We both told him about Heidelberg. I was there – or have you forgotten?'

'No. I mean I texted him a few minutes ago and told him that I had never left Pocklington, and that I had moved out in order to try to stop drinking. I think he got it.'

'You told him that because you thought he might be bored on the train? Because being threatened at gunpoint is just not enough to keep his mind occupied?'

'I told him because I wanted him to know the truth.'

'Before he gets shot?'

'Don't say that, Celia.'

'I can't help it.' I can hear more swigging from the wine bottle, and then a prolonged, masculine, polyphonic burp, and then some fumbling, and finally a cork popping, and an effusion. 'Oh, shit! I'll meet you in The George.'

'What?'

'In the George. I'll meet you. I can't stand to be alone anymore. I know I threw you out. Well, now I'm throwing you back in again.'

'That's wonderful, Celia, but not in The George.'

'Where, then? The Three Feathers? God, you're picky.'

'No, Celia. I mean I'd be overjoyed to meet you, but it can't be in a pub. I'm not ready to go to a place where they serve alcohol, yet. I'd just be setting myself up to fail. Can I just come home?'

'Yes. Does me necking bottles of warm Cava count as "serving alcohol"?'

'No, silly. It doesn't.'

'Good. Come round then. I mean, come home, then.'

I hear a sound suggestive of something falling and the call is cut.

I'm just getting a few things together when I get another text message. It's from Bradley's phone.

> 8 December 2012 11:28
> Dad, the man seems to be getting wound up. I don't think he believes I'm asleep any more. Going to turn the ringer on my phone back on, and I want you to call me. I'll pretend to wake up, then I want you to talk to me. Don't ask me why, but I think he'll be less jumpy if he sees me talking on the phone. Another thing. Again, don't ask why. Can you speak to me in German, please? It's important. Also, can you talk as if you are an Allied secret agent in a black and

white film about World War Two.
Escape from Colditz and stuff.

I call Bradley's phone.

'Fritz hier. Wer ist am apparat, bitte?' Bradley answers.

'Ah, Fritz. How goes it? You are on the train?' I say to him in German.

'Yes, on the train. I have before me another comrade who needs to go on holiday in Switzerland.'

'Ah. ' I'm struggling to think of things to say, but I want to give Bradley a prompt if I can. 'I hear the weather is good in Switzerland at this time of year.' I am hoping that Bradley will understand what I am saying, but I know he will. He moaned like anything when his mother had the idea of getting him a German tutor, but he still applied himself to the lessons.

'But of course. This comrade is well prepared. He has much equipment,' Bradley replies.

'I approve. We are always short of equipment. Fate helps those who help themselves. Can you list the items of his equipment?'

'Just so. He has passport, clothing, groceries, and map. This comrade desires to disembark from the transport at what I believe to be a bad location,' Says Bradley. He speaks slowly, as if choosing his words carefully. 'In Kings Cross.' He says the last two words in English.

'Oh, Thou Dear Time! Can we support this?'

'I have a simple idea,' says Bradley, more brightly. 'The comrade could instead disembark at the place before, where he will be safe, I think.'

'Can our friend hear what we are saying? If he can hear, can our friend understand what we are saying?'

This isn't just playing along with Bradley's game: it is something I want to find out.

'I do not know. It does not matter.'

'Can I have permission to say something?' I ask Bradley, still in German.

'What? Yes. By all means.'

'The Committee thinks very highly of this agent. The agent is likely to obtain a medal upon completion of the mission.'

'Keep calm. There is still much to be done. Can I put our friend on the phone?'

'Repeat message please. Not understood.' What? Surely Bradley can't mean that I have to speak to the nutter.

'The comrade opposite me. Can I put him on the apparatus to speak to you?'

'Er. Yes. Yes, of course.'

I put the phone on mute for a few seconds and I utter the following prayer: *please please please please please don't let my son be shot or harmed in any way. I will stay off alcohol and I will not exploit my naive wife even if she lets me move back home again and I will diligently attempt a reconciliation with my daughter even though she is the only person who has ever seen through me but please don't let Bradley be shot on his own on a train.*

I have what Celia's therapist would insist on calling, 'a moment of lucidity'. Bradley has realised that the crucial thing is to get off the train, and to get himself out of the situation where he is sitting opposite a nutter whose unbalanced mind is occupied by thoughts of nothing other than when he might shoot Bradley. It is going to seem much more natural to the nutter to let Bradley off if the nutter is getting off the train himself at the same stop.

In very slow, clear German, I say, 'Hello. Who is there?'

'I am called Karl-Heinz Weber,' says the nutter, in a very poor German accent.

'Hello, Karl-Heinz Weber. How are you?'

'I am OK. I need to get to Basel.'

'That is no problem. I can help you get to Basel.'

'Ah, good.'

'My friend tells me that the ticket you hold is for Kings Cross. Is that right?'

'Yes.'

'OK. Our information is that you should not get off the train at Kings Cross. It would be bad for you. You should get off the train at Stevenage, which is the stop before. You know Stevenage?'

'Yes, I know Stevenage.'

'Good. You and my friend should get off the train separately. Not together. Not from the same door. But you should both get off the train at Stevenage. Do you understand?'

'I understand.'

'After you get off the train, you and my friend should stay as far apart as possible. Do you agree?'

'I agree. Thank you.'

'Goodbye.'

'Goodbye.'

The nutter hangs up the phone. I stop thinking in German.

I am The Dad.

I briefly consider calling the police and telling them to expect the nutter at Stevenage instead of Kings Cross, but I don't.

5. Suspect Device

THE TRAIN STOPS for a long time just outside Stevenage station. I press my forehead against the window, to see if I can spot my grandpa on the platform, but it is too far away. Something seems to be wrong. It should not take this long to get into a station where the train is due to stop.

'This is a customer announcement. We regret to inform passengers that a suspicious package has been found on a platform at Stevenage. For this reason, this service will pass straight through Stevenage station, and passengers who wanted to disembark at Stevenage should leave the train at London Kings Cross, and await further information.'

I glance at Herr Weber, and I can tell that he is angry. He takes the Luger out of his inside pocket and points it at me again.

'You want to give me to the Nazis,' he says in German.

'On the contrary, I am against the Nazis. I want to help you to escape.' I am racking my brains to remember all my extra German lessons. I will need to buy my mum a bunch of flowers if I ever get out of this.

The train moves on again, and goes through Stevenage station at full speed. I don't know how much longer I have got to live. The train is supposed to be in Kings Cross in twenty-six minutes. I need to call my dad again.

I am just about to call him, when my phone rings. I don't recognise the number. It is another mobile, but not one in my contacts list. Without thinking, I answer it.

'Hello?'

'BRADLEY? ARE YOU THERE?' The voice is so loud that I don't recognise it at first. I take the phone away from my ear and press the button to reduce the volume on the speaker. 'BRADLEY? ARE YOU THERE, LAD?' the voice keeps saying. Herr Weber frowns even more, and fidgets. He starts tapping the edge of the table with his fingertips and breathing out very loudly.

'Hello?' I say. This time, the voice is not ear-splitting and I can recognise who it is.

'Bradley. This is your grandpa. Where are you? I'm in the station, outside the main entrance. Which platform are you on?'

'I'm still on the train, grandpa.'

'When does the train get into Stevenage?'

'It has already gone through Stevenage. It didn't stop.'

'I think there's some problem with the trains. They won't let me inside the station.'

'Yes, I know. That's why I am still on the train.'

'So where is the train, now?'

'On the way to London.'

'Oh, bloody hell. Do you want me to come and meet you in London?'

'No thanks, grandpa. I'll call you again when I get off the train, when I've got more information.'

'Your grandma's expecting us back for tea. There'll be hell to pay if we're late.'

'Yes, grandpa. I'm sorry. I'll call you back later.'

I end the call. I look at Herr Weber, not straight in the eye, but closely enough to try to work out if he's going to do anything. I look at my watch. There's nineteen more minutes until we get to Kings Cross. Herr Weber is holding one side of his coat with his left hand, and has his right hand inside the coat, as if holding onto the Luger. He looks calmer than a few minutes ago, but he also looks as if he is trying to make his mind up about something. I tell myself to stop looking at my watch.

The door of the carriage opens and a man in a dark blue uniform appears. He is one of the train crew. He glances at Herr Weber. He glances at me. I realise that I really need the toilet. The uniformed man sits down in one of two empty seats on the other side of the aisle from Herr Weber. He is tall and well-built: so tall that his knees are pressing against the seat in front of him. He looks surly. He has very short hair and a funny kind of dark green tattoo in the space between his thumb and index finger on one hand. He has one of those clip-on polyester ties and things like keys and identification cards hanging round his neck on pieces of multi-coloured tape.

Herr Weber looks at the uniformed man, and then looks at me, and then looks down at the table. He pulls his right hand out from the inside of his coat. We sit there for what seems like hours. I let myself look at my watch again. Another six minutes, and we will arrive in London. I wonder how much Herr Weber knows about the timetable. He doesn't seem to have a watch on.

The train waits for a platform at Kings Cross. There is an announcement, which goes on about passengers for Stevenage, but I don't catch any of what it says. The other passengers get out of their seats and bump into each other and say sorry and start getting their stuff together. My suitcase is on the rack above me, but I don't move. Herr Weber doesn't move. The man in the blue uniform watches us.

The other passengers start to form queues near the doors. Two or three go past us and then I can hear them talking.

'What's the matter?'

'We need to go into the next carriage. Or back to the other end of this carriage.'

'Why?'

'This door is out of order.'

Just as the train is rolling to a stop, the man in the blue uniform gets up and sits down next to Herr Weber. He takes up so much room that Herr Weber has to move as near to the window as he can get. Herr Weber looks pale. He grips the edge of the table. His head is shaking.

I hear a strange noise, like a loud crackle. The man in the blue uniform takes a radio out of his pocket and says something into it. All I catch is the word 'over' at the end.

The doors bleep, and then open. Everybody except us gets off. Herr Weber looks at the man, but the man's face is expressionless. I start to get up. I don't want to get up. I seem to do it by accident, because everybody else is getting off the train.

'Remain seated, please, sir,' says the man. I don't remember being called 'sir' before. I do as he tells me, but then I don't know what I am supposed to do once I sit down again. I don't know where to look, or whether to try to talk, or what is going to happen next. I can't even decide if I feel cold or hot. I keep thinking the uniformed man is going to ask for my ticket.

Someone knocks on the window so hard that it takes me a moment to work out what caused the noise. With the shock it is all I can do to stop myself from crying. For a few seconds, I think I am going to wet myself. It sounded as if whoever it was hit the window with a hammer but, when I look round, all I see is a policeman and another man in a train company uniform standing on the platform. The uniformed man inside beckons them. They do something to one of the doors and it opens.

I'm on the platform. I don't feel well. The train company man and another policeman are asking me things, and I'm replying, but I can't really understand what they are asking me, or what I am saying. All I know is that it is in English. It feels difficult to find the right words in English.

'But he did threaten you, didn't he?'

'Sort of.' They look annoyed. I think I really am going to cry. I'm even more desperate for the toilet.

'What did he do?'

'He pointed a Luger at me.' They say things into their radios.

I can see Herr Weber through the window of the train. They are putting handcuffs on him, and escorting him onto the platform. One of the policemen has a plastic bag with labels on it containing some things which I guess must have belonged to Herr Weber.

Somebody is leading me slowly along the platform. I can hear a policeman talking behind me into his radio.

'Yes. Pretty harmless, if you ask me. The gun is a real Luger, and the ammunition is live. But the gun is 7.65 millimetre and the rounds are 9 millimetre, which perhaps explains why the gun wasn't loaded. Also, it looks as if it hasn't been cleaned since the Battle of the Bulge. What else? A duffle-bag containing assorted tinned food, a length of washing-line, one pair of tin-snippers, an old-fashioned-looking map of Europe, some play money, a...

what? Yes. Play money. No, I don't think we'll be asking the CPS to do him for forgery. And a thing that looks like a passport out of a kid's comic, with the name Karl-Heinz Webber on it and a date of birth of first of March, 1914. No, he is not ninety-eight years old. I would have said he is in his mid-to-late fifties. We also found a library card with the name Arthur Crannis. Oh, and a framed, black and white photograph of a woman and two children in the garden of a country cottage. Would you believe he had a valid ticket? Yes, I would have put money on it as well. The kid? He's still in one piece. I'll ask the paramedics to have a look at him. He does look a bit iffy. What? Bradley Martin Crichton. Yes, I've contacted his next of kin.'

They are taking me somewhere, but I am not sure where. I can see two policemen leading Herr Weber out of the station. A third policeman is carrying the plastic bag. I shout, 'Viel Glück, Herr Weber!' but I don't think he can hear me.

After I've finished with the paramedic and been to the toilet and feel a bit calmer, I look for somewhere to sit while I call my mum and tell her that I don't want to go to grandpa and grandma's. I just want to go home.

The author acknowledges the invaluable support, expertise and guidance of the following people: Michael Stewart, Gaia Holmes, Claire Jones, Steve Potter, Joanna Crosby, Matt O'Brien, Jane Lockwood, Jared Exley, and Valerie Anderson.